To my veggie-lovin' boys who never fail to get
their broccoli super powers.
-S.C.

To my healthy, creative, supportive family!
-G.H.

The Boy Who Loved Broccoli

by Sarah A. Creighton
Illustrated by Gene L. Hamilton
Print Work & Editing by Dave Thrasher

VK Publishing
vkpublishinginc@gmail.com
California

The Boy
Who Loved
Broccoli

by Sarah Creighton

Illustrated by Gene L. Hamilton

Once upon a time there was a very ordinary boy who lived in a very ordinary house in a very ordinary city. His name was Baxter and he loved to eat vegetables, especially broccoli! Broccoli was his very favorite.

One normal afternoon, he asked his mom if she would
please fix him a large plate of the yummy green veggies.

He sat down at the usual kitchen table and started to eat and eat and EAT! Baxter had never tasted anything so scrumptious! This wasn't the same full feeling he had felt the last time he ate broccoli.

As he ate, he felt as though something strange was happening. He began to notice that with each bite he took, his clothes felt tighter and tighter. But he kept on eating because his broccoli was so delicious!

Soon Baxter noticed that the same kitchen table and chair where he always sat began to appear smaller and smaller. But really he was getting bigger, much bigger.

Rapidly, his head touched the ceiling and with every bite of broccoli he grew larger and stronger than ever before. Baxter's body was filling up fast with super powers from the broccoli he was eating!

The boy realized he could do anything. He was as big and as strong as a dinosaur! He had super hero power! This ordinary day was turning out to be not so ordinary after all.... extraordinary, in fact! Completely amazed by his new power and strength, Baxter tore through the roof of his house and began to run... FAST!!

He jumped over freeways and
ran past skyscrapers; splashed
through lakes and leaped over mountains.
He wasn't even out of breath!

Baxter spent most of the afternoon running free, experiencing his new-found powers. As he was wondering what a superhero with such strength could do, he heard someone calling for help. This was his chance to use his superhero powers!

He followed the cry for help and discovered a girl whose kite was caught in a tall tree. She stood at the bottom of the tree trunk looking up through the lofty branches at her stuck kite when Baxter appeared. "I'll help you get your kite!", Baxter said to the girl whose eyes were filled with tears. Shocked at the sight of the giant, the girl just stood with her mouth wide open.

"Do you have any broccoli at your house?", Baxter asked the girl. "Go get some - QUICK!" The girl, too afraid to ask why, ran into her house and came back with a stalk of broccoli. She handed it to Baxter. Baxter shook his head and told her to take a bite. As she did, she grew a bit taller. He told her to take another bite and another.

Soon the girl was almost the size of Baxter, filled with super broccoli powers! Now she could simply reach over and easily grab her kite from the tallest tree branch. "How did you know..", the girl began to ask Baxter. But before she could finish her question, he pointed to the broccoli and whispered, "Eat your broccoli and you'll see, you will be as big as me." He gave her a wink and darted off.

So pleased with his superhero good deed, he wanted to find more people to help. That afternoon, Baxter helped an old man whose heavy boxes fell from his truck,

a kindergarten class whose recess ball was across a busy street, and a boy whose bicycle wheel was tangled on the railroad track. After he helped each person, he made sure to whisper the secret to them, "Eat your broccoli and you'll see, you will be as big as me."

What a day! Baxter began to feel a bit tired and started to head back, but he had traveled so far with his super broccoli powers that he was very, very far from home. Upon his journey back, he noticed that with each step he took, he grew shorter and smaller.

Because Baxter was hungry, he was losing his superhero powers and started shrinking back to his normal size again.

After walking and running for some time, Baxter began to worry that he might not make it home before dark. He suddenly felt scared for the first time all day. While he rested by a tree, he put his head in his hands and began to cry.

Feeling the ground shake, Baxter looked up from his tears. There, standing before him, was the girl with the kite, the old man with the boxes, the kindergartners with the ball, and the boy with the bicycle. Only this time, they were towering over **him**!

"Wh-wh-what are you all doing here? And why do you all look so big and strong?", Baxter wondered aloud.

In unison,
they replied,
"eat your broccoli
and you'll see,
you will be as big as me!"

Everyone Baxter had helped that afternoon heard his cry and came back to help him. The group told Baxter that the word had spread about broccoli having super powers and they wanted to thank him as they helped him find his way back home. They even discussed meeting up together the following day to use their super powers to help more people. Baxter and his new friends decided they would conquer the world, one broccoli stalk at a time!

When Baxter returned home and walked in the doorway, his mom wondered where he had been and why his clothes were torn. With his stomach growling, Baxter wondered if it had all just been a part of his imagination.

Giving his mom a hug, he asked her what was for dinner. She replied...

"Broccoli!"
Uh-oh!

Broccoli Fun Facts:

 Broccoli is part of the cruciferous family of vegetables. Try saying that one five times fast!

 Broccoli is a good source of fiber. Can you think of anything that rhymes with fiber? Neither can we...

 Broccoli is full of calcium-good for your bones! And you need strong bones to be a super hero, right?

 Broccoli is rich in vitamins A & C...which stand for Awesome & Cool!

 Eating a diet rich in broccoli gives you superpowers. Okay, maybe that one can't officially be proven but we believe it!